Red Ridinghood's Little Lamb

Charlotte Steiner

Red Ridinghood's Little Lamb

Alfred A. Knopf

New York

L. C. catalog card number: 63-21812

This is a Borzoi Book, published by Alfred A. Knopf, Inc.

Red Ridinghood's Little Lamb

Red Ridinghood was an only child. She lived with her parents on the edge of a meadow that was deep in the forest. There were no other children to play with her. This made her a very lonely little girl.

One of her favorite all-by-herself games was marbles. She would play first on one side of the ring, and then the other. Sometimes she would win a game, and sometimes her pretend self would win a game.

Her father and mother decided she needed a pet of her very own to play with. Fido, the dog, could not play with her, for he was a watchdog and had to guard the house. Minnie, the cat, liked to hunt by herself and had no time for games.

On the day before Easter, Red Ridinghood's father journeyed down the road and over the hills to the nearest farmer. When he returned in the evening, he had a little lamb in his arms.

Mother put a tinkling bell on a ribbon and tied it around the lamb's neck. Then she lined a covered basket with soft hay to make a warm bed for the little pet.

The next morning, Red Ridinghood ran outside to search for Easter eggs. Under a bush she found the basket. "I'm sure this is for me," she thought. "Perhaps the basket is filled with Easter eggs."

She lifted the cover. Instead of bright, colored eggs, she saw a white lamb.

"Mother, mother," Red Ridinghood called, "look what I have found. The Easter Bunny left a real lamb for me."

Her mother smiled. "Now you have a friend who can run and play with you."

Sometimes the lamb and Red Ridinghood played hide-and-seek. Sometimes they played tag. And sometimes they played both games at once. Ridinghood did not have to play all-by-herself games anymore. She all but forgot about marbles.

One day the lamb scampered across the meadow to the edge of the wood. Red Ridinghood followed her pet. As she reached the meadow's end, the lamb dashed into the forest. Red Ridinghood could not see her lamb any longer, but she could still hear its bell. She followed the tinkling sound deeper and deeper into the forest,

until . . . .

Behind a large rock she saw a tiny man in a peaked cap holding the lamb and singing:

"Three and three and three are nine;
This white lamb is now all mine."

Red Ridinghood rushed up to the tiny man. "The lamb is not yours. It's mine," she said. "The Easter Bunny left it for me."

But the dwarf kept holding the lamb and singing:

"Three and three and three are nine;
This white lamb is now all mine."

Red Ridinghood tried to pick up her lamb. But the dwarf had cast a spell. An invisible wall was between her hand and the lamb. She could not force her way through. She sat down on a nearby stone and began to cry.

The dwarf put his hands up to his ears. Red Ridinghood cried louder than before.

"Stop crying," the dwarf said. "You are making my ears hurt."

But Red Ridinghood could not stop.

"All right," said the little man, "if you will promise to stop crying, I will take you to my master. He will decide who should have the lamb."

Red Ridinghood stopped crying and followed the dwarf.

Carrying the lamb, the dwarf led Red Ridinghood to a mountain way in the middle of the forest. Hidden in the mountainside was the entrance to a cave. Red Ridinghood and the little man walked down steps and steps and more steps, deeper and deeper into the mountain. A soft, glowing light shone in the cave. There were bushes covered with berries along the passageway.

At the end of the steps was a door. When they opened the

door, they were in a large hall. It was filled with dwarfs who were busy cutting and polishing pieces of rock.

The Master Dwarf was seated on a big, wooden chair. He saw Red Ridinghood and her companion standing in the doorway.

"Well, Pebbles," he said to the little man, "you are late again. Where have you been? Who is this little girl? And why are you carrying a lamb?"

Red Ridinghood stepped forward. "I am Red Ridinghood, sir. The lamb was my gift from the Easter Bunny. Please may I have it back?"

"No, no, no!" Pebbles screamed. "It's mine. I found it. Finders-keepers. Tell her! Tell her! I sang the dwarf song:

> Three and three and three are nine;
> This white lamb is now all mine."

By now all the other dwarfs had stopped work to listen.

"Finders-keepers *is* a dwarf law," the Master Dwarf said softly to Red Ridinghood.

At that, Red Ridinghood started to cry again. All the kindly dwarfs were distressed—except Pebbles, who held his hands over his ears.

The Master Dwarf spoke again. "Well, it *is* a dwarf law—but Red Ridinghood is not a dwarf. Therefore, dwarf law does not apply. We shall have to have a contest. They will play a game, and the winner shall have the lamb. Red Ridinghood, you shall choose the game."

Red Ridinghood, still crying softly said, "Tag and hide-and-seek are the only games I know how to play. Oh, and marbles."

"Marbles is best," said the Master Dwarf.

Red Ridinghood stopped crying. "But I don't want to play marbles. I just want my little white lamb."

"Patience. Patience," said the Master Dwarf. "Fair is fair." And he opened a big sack that was standing in the corner of the room. It was as though a bright light had been turned on. The sack was filled with glittering marbles all colors of the rainbow. They were made of stones shaped and polished by the dwarfs, the loveliest marbles Red Ridinghood had ever seen.

Pebbles grinned. He was very sure that he would win. He was the second-best marble player of all the dwarfs.

Red Ridinghood dried her tears. Oh, she would do her best—but was her best good enough? She hadn't played marbles for a while, not since she had gotten her lamb. And she had never played marbles with another person before, only her pretend self. Would her best be good enough?

Pebbles and Red Ridinghood were each given a bowl of marbles and the game began.

Pebbles was winning at first. But everytime he won a marble, the dwarfs booed. They didn't like Pebbles. The booing made him nervous. He put his hands over his ears.

Whenever Red Ridinghood scored, the dwarfs cheered and clapped their hands. Red Ridinghood had never had anyone cheer for her before. The more the dwarfs cheered, the better she became. She won one marble. Then another. Then a third. Pretty soon she had won all of Pebbles's marbles!

The Master Dwarf brought the lamb over to Red Riding-hood. "The lamb belongs to you," he said. "Fair is fair."

The lamb bumped her shoulder and said, "Baa, baa."

Red Ridinghood wanted to put the marbles she had won back into the big sack. But the Master Dwarf said, "The marbles belong to you. Fair is fair."

Red Ridinghood was overjoyed. She had never had such beautiful marbles.

Then the dwarfs escorted her to a secret door at the other end of the hall. With the lamb in her arms, Red Ridinghood stepped onto a big, flat rock. The dwarfs pulled on a rope, and the rock began to rise. In no time at all, Red Ridinghood and the lamb were at the top of a long shaft. Red Ridinghood stepped off the rock and found herself in the woods, quite near her home.

When her mother saw the little bag of marbles, she wondered where Red Ridinghood had found them. She thought that the kindly woodsman might have given them to her.

Red Ridinghood began to tell her mother the story of the marbles. "You know the pine woods near the big rock. . . ." she said. Just then, the lamb started to run towards the meadow's edge.

"Tell you later," Red Ridinghood called to her mother and quickly ran to catch the lamb. She had to reach it before it ran away into the forest again.

Text set in Monotype Baskerville. Composed at Westcott and Thomson, Philadelphia. Printed by Reehl Litho, New York City. Bound by Economy Bookbinding Corp., Kearny, N. J. Typography by Atha Tehon.